The Little Sex Shop Around the Corner

Em Taylor

Published by Em Taylor, 2016.

Edited by: Em Petrova

This is a work of fiction. Similarities to real people, places, or events are entirely coincidental.

THE LITTLE SEX SHOP AROUND THE CORNER

First edition. May 10, 2016.

Written by Em Taylor.

Chapter 1

SHE HATED THESE DAMNED meetings, but it was business suicide not to attend, even if she had become the local Small Business Association's very own pariah. She was just going to have to suck it up.

And so, Cassidy Moore took a deep, steadying breath and pushed the door to enter the large conference room of Strathmorris Town Hall. The building was a typical nineteen seventies structure, decorated in a job lot of light blue-grey paint, dark green industrial carpeting and gloss skirting that was a shade of brown that polite people did not attempt to describe.

But Cassidy still loved the old building. She had danced in her first ballet shows here, watched her first pantomimes here and voted in her first election within these hallowed walls.

But today it was the place where she would be judged and found wanting—where peers would look down their noses at her because she was trying to make a little extra money in tough times. Because she thought that grown adults should have the right to make their own choices and should be able to buy certain products for use in their own bedrooms, and that she should be able to turn a profit from that gap in the market. But God forbid that she should do that, even when a chain of newsagents sold an entire top shelf of magazines of nude women and readers wives story magazines and everyone knew fine what went on at the Electra Lounge after hours.

"HEY THERE, YOU LOOK about as bored as I am."

Cassidy looked up into hazel eyes that gleamed with mischief. She had been staring forlornly at the range of finger food on her paper plate and wondering what kind of topping to get on her pizza on the way home. She tried for a smile but suspected she produced a grimace.

"Ah yes, I'm afraid so. I was expecting a little controversy tonight but it seems to be the same boring old sods going on and on about business rates and the problem of litter in the town centre. You must be new if you were expecting cut and thrust business deals."

"Gavin Wallace. I'm not new to town. I grew up here but I am new to the Small Business Association." The dark-haired stranger stuck out his hand. Cassidy laid down her plastic cup and gripped it. His handshake was warm and firm. The warmth moved up her arm and down her torso, settling in her groin. Bloody hell! He was good-looking and sexy. And he had a kind smile. Either he didn't know that she was the notorious sex shop owner or he didn't care. She hoped it was the latter.

He was wearing a charcoal grey suit. She didn't know a lot about men's clothing but it was obviously an expensive suit. There was something about the cut of it and the way it hung from his broad shoulders. His tie was a deep purple, which looked elegant over his crisp white shirt. The thin silver tie pin set off his look perfectly. It was a shame he would soon find out who she was. She'd bet he was an accountant or a banker or something else equally dull. Not because he was dull-looking but because he was so smart. And besides, he had money.

"I'm Cassidy Moore. I own a boutique in Cressham Lane."

"Oh cool. I'm about to start a business in the high street just around the corner from Cressham Lane. I bought the old record shop."

"Vinyl Vixens? Oh I loved that shop when I was growing up. It didn't seem to matter that they mainly sold CDs. What kind of shop are you planning to open?"

"A comic book store."

She cocked an eyebrow. Huh! So she'd totally misread that play. "Fantastic. Just the type of place that will draw the young ones in from the out-of-town retail park."

"What kind of boutique do you have? Women's clothes I take it."

"Well, umm, yeah. It's lingerie really."

"Nice. I won't have cause to come into your shop to purchase unfortunately since I don't have a girlfriend, but maybe we could have coffee some time."

"That would be nice." Frankly she'd be happy to have a lot more than coffee with him. But who was she kidding? Once Mr Suave, Cool and Sophisticated found out about the rest of the goods in her shop he'd be heading for the hills. Shame. He reminded her a bit of Henry Cavill in *Man of Steel*.

"Ms Moore, we were wondering if you could spare us a few minutes." The nasal tones of the President of the Small Business Association broke into her thoughts as she thought of Gavin Wallace in a Superman costume. It was quite a nice vision.

She snapped her head up and frowned at the fat, balding little man, with piggy eyes and a snout for a nose. It wouldn't come as a shock to anyone to find out the man was a butcher.

Here goes. She had known this moment would come. Every meeting for the last few months they had urged her to remove her new line of sex toys from her shop. But she had bought the toys on a no-returns contract. The wholesalers had refused to consider a sale or return option, so she had to sell them. And they were selling well. Maybe she could remove them from her shop and sell them on ebay, but part of her was stubborn. They were sex toys, for heaven's sake. She wasn't selling crystal meth to teenagers at the back of her little boutique.

"I'm sorry," she said to the president. "I would love to stay and chat, but I'm afraid I have a dentist appointment." She couldn't help herself. She had to come up with the most ridiculous excuse so that he knew that she was lying, and thus refusing to talk to them, yet again, about why she would continue to sell vibrators and blow-up dolls.

"At this time?" asked Mr Jones incredulously.

"It's amazing, isn't it? All-night dentists. What will they think of next?" Cassidy looked up at Gavin as he said this. He was playing along. The hint of a smile quirked his lips and she had to purse her own lips to stop herself from bursting out laughing. "Come on, dear. I said I'd hold your hand as you get your filling." He placed his hand on her shoulder and guided her towards the door.

Once they were outside, they both burst out laughing. Cassidy bent over and held onto her knees as she fought for breath and to compose herself again. He chuckled heartily. When she straightened, his laughter died and his smile waned slightly. They stood for just a moment too long, looking into each other's eyes.

"Best get you to the dentist then." His grin was back as he rummaged in his coat pocket and produced car keys.

"You know I was lying, don't you?"

"Yeah, I know. I thought I'd take you to Starbucks, if you fancy a coffee?"

Her eyes narrowed suspiciously as she contemplated his offer. Starbucks was a couple of miles away and she didn't know him.

Oh, what the hell. The chances of him being a crazy axe murderer were pretty slim and even if he did kill her, at least the last thing she would see was a really cute guy. She shrugged and walked towards the car with the flashing hazard lights.

Chapter 2

GAVIN COULDN'T BELIEVE his luck. Cassidy was gorgeous. She had long brown hair, a curvaceous body with a decent set of hips that you could grab hold of and a sweet smile with a pouty bottom lip. He could feel his cock harden as he watched her. Between her nervous gesture of licking her bottom lip and running her top teeth over it and her emerald eyes, he was struggling to maintain his composure. Her eyes were so green, he wondered if she had some kind of contacts in.

But it wasn't just in the looks department that Cassidy was head and shoulders above most girls he met. She owned her own business and seemed quite clever, though she wasn't giving much of herself away.

She was also normal. Gavin so wanted to meet normal women with normal goals, not the London set who attended Henley Regatta and Royal Ascot and thought you were a nobody if you hadn't been invited to the Royal Wedding. He had been invited to the Royal Wedding and he'd attended, but he didn't feel the need to tell everyone he knew.

Cassidy made talking easier. She led the conversation all the way to Starbucks—something he generally sucked at. Normally people with such a privileged upbringing as he'd had were confident in any social gathering but not Gavin. He had been sent to Eton where he had been bullied for his uncouth Scottish accent, then forced to go to Oxford to complete a degree and then an MBA. He'd hated every minute of his five years working in a bank, saving every penny to allow him to open his comic book store.

Even tonight, trussed up in a shirt and tie and an Armani suit, he felt like a fraud. He couldn't wait to get home and don jeans and a t-shirt. He tugged at his tie, used to the stricture but still feeling as if the noose was tightening around his throat.

Gavin's real friends consisted of people he had met on the internet, and who he met up with at comic cons and conventions. He only saw them about one weekend a month but he spoke to them every day on Facebook and Twitter. The people he quaffed champagne with on the other Friday nights in Edinburgh's posh wine bars were mere colleagues. And now they were not even that.

When he had left the bank, his father had threatened to cut him off without a penny. But Gavin knew this was an idle threat. He was an only child and his father was very rich, having made a number of very savvy investments during the economic boom years. He played the stock market extremely well. He also lived off his income and expenses from being the local Member of Parliament.

Gavin had called his father's bluff and gone ahead anyway, taken on the lease of the shop and bought as much decent stock as possible.

And now here he was, driving Cassidy back to town in his Mercedes. She looked suitably impressed. There was something to be said for having money, after all.

"Sooo, I know this is a bit forward, but you've obviously got money... Why a comic book store?"

He stole a glance at her as he slowed down for a set of traffic lights. "I like comic books."

"Hmm, well that puts me in my place."

"What do you mean?" He half-turned. They had about a minute until these particular lights changed.

"Well, you just basically told me to mind my own business. It's fine. It was rude to ask."

"No, I didn't mean to. I genuinely like comic books and the movies and TV programmes that go along with them."

"But it's the kind of thing teenage boys like."

"They say men never really grow up." He turned back to the steering wheel. How much was he willing to reveal to this girl he had just met? In Starbucks they learned about each other on a superficial level. Cassidy didn't seem keen to talk about her business, but maybe she just preferred to separate work and pleasure. He avoided the topic of his background for obvious reasons. So they'd stuck to books, music and films.

He'd been entranced. He'd wanted to touch her and move the errant strand of hair that kept falling in front of her eyes back behind her ear. He could see the outline of her bra under the thin material of her blouse. He wanted to see what lay beneath. As she spoke, he'd watched her lips and wondered how soft they would be against his own.

She angled her body toward him the best she could in his car. "So you're really just an overgrown teenager with a big fancy car?"

"Yes... no. I went to Eton." He paused to let that sink in. Everyone in the UK knew that Eton was the most exclusive boy's boarding school and that you had to be extremely rich to go there. "I hated it. So whenever I could, I'd go into Windsor and Eton and go around all the second-hand shops and see if they had any old comics. They invariably did. It was amazing the stuff these old shops got their hands on. I became a dab hand at spotting the good stuff. In my holidays I'd go to comic cons. When I wasn't out on the rugby pitch or at some other school club, I was watching videos of Superman, Spiderman, Batman etc. I became a geek. Partly out of loneliness."

He was now negotiating a busy roundabout.

"But you look really smart, like a proper business man. Not like me."

"I fill out a suit OK but I prefer jeans."

"Did you tell your parents you hated school?"

"My Dad didn't want to know. He loves me but he went to Eton so that's where I had to go. He's as rich as Croesus, so that's the way things have to be."

"Who or what is Croesus?" she asked. He turned and looked at her open expression. He liked that she was not embarrassed to ask.

"An ancient Perisan king who was known for his wealth. It's just an expression."

She chuckled. "Maybe in Eton, but not in Strathmorris."

He barked out a laugh. "No, perhaps not. I wasn't trying to show off."

"I know." She sounded genuine. "But you have friends now?"

"Oh yes. Everything's fine now." And it was. Now he was following his dream.

He parked outside his shop and turned to her, not wanting the evening to end. He knew she lived just around the corner. She had explained to him that she lived in the little flat above her own shop. Perhaps he could convince her to stay out a little while longer.

"Would you do me a favour and come into the shop and tell me what you think?" he asked.

"Yeah, sure."

Cassidy would be the first person to see his shop apart from the shop fitters and painters whom he had hired. His father had told him he was not remotely interested in his hobbies and would be no help anyway. He unset the alarm and switched on the light—a knot of worry growing in his stomach. What if it was rubbish?

She blinked. "Oh, I like it. You don't think of a comic book store as being so clean and well-organised."

"I didn't want to put people off who are not particularly geeky but who like the types of programmes and films that are made into comic books."

"Good idea. But it's a bit... well... it's a bit bare."

"I have a load of point of sale material from my suppliers and a big bundle of posters, but I'm not really sure which ones to put up. I don't want it to get too crowded."

"Where are they all?"

"In the back shop." He pointed to the door behind the small coffee bar.

"I'll know where to come when I need a latte during my work day." She grinned, heading over to the door.

They spent an hour picking out point of sale items and posters and another one setting them around the shop and putting up the posters. By the end, he had discarded his jacket and tie and his crisp white shirt was covered in dust.

"I think that will do," Cassidy said, stepping back from a display of Spiderman books. She had draped pretend spider web over the holder and a large cardboard cut-outs of Spiderman appeared to be scaling the walls of the shop. It looked great.

"Fantastic," he breathed walking up beside her and turning to face her. She smiled up at him—the smudge of dirt on the side of her nose making her look even cuter. He fished in his pocket for a handkerchief and wiped her face with it gently. His cock started to harden as he imagined stripping off her smart shirt and leather skirt. He could see a hint of cleavage. His hand itched to cup her breasts. Her cheeks had turned pink. Was she turned on or embarrassed for him trying to make a move on her?

Cassidy suddenly lifted herself onto her tiptoes and pressed a delicate kiss on his lips. Then she stepped back. He wanted to grab her ass and press her against his hardening cock, but he didn't want to scare her away.

"I have to be up early in the morning. Have a good day tomorrow, because when you open on Friday, it's going to be hectic."

"Have dinner with me tomorrow." His blurted request sounded desperate. Damn. So much for the suave, sophisticated business man. "Please!" Oh God, now he was pleading.

"OK. I'll be here about six." She winked, grabbed her coat from the counter and disappeared through the door. The tinkle of the bell made him shake his head. Shit. He should have offered to walk her home. What was wrong with him? He placed his hand over his hard cock and squeezed. He knew exactly what was wrong with him. He was thinking with his penis. Unfortunately, he liked the ideas that his penis was coming up with.

Chapter 3

IT HAD BEEN A RELATIVELY busy morning considering that it was only Wednesday. But it was also a week until Valentine's Day and the shop did tend to get a little busier as boyfriends and husbands attempted to work out the size their other half took in lingerie. Her assistant, Danni was always a treat to watch. She was placing a rather red-faced young man's hand onto her breast.

"Bigger or smaller than that?"

"Maybe a little bit smaller. Kind of a good handful but not too much."

"Sounds like a B-cup to me."

Cassidy smiled to herself and looked back at the order she was filling out. For all the local business community, the churches and a number of moral high-grounders objected, the rest of the town seemed to be happy that she was selling sex toys. They were very popular and she had been surprised by the large range of people who had come into the shop looking for toys to enhance their sex life.

She looked out the window for what must have been the hundredth time that morning and wondered what Gavin Wallace was doing. Was he just around the corner in his new shop? Maybe he was out at a wholesalers getting more stock, or taking advantage of his last days of freedom before becoming a proper business owner. She had been very impressed with his décor and layout and even more impressed that he had been willing to take advice. Not many people would have accepted help from a virtual stranger. But then, they had got on so well. She had sensed a real spark of attraction between them.

Oh, who the hell was she trying to kid? Attraction? Her pussy had been aching since they'd arrived at Starbucks, probably before. She'd wanted to jump him all night and she'd had to force herself to make that kiss nothing more than a peck him, tempting as it may have been to wrap herself around him and rut against him like an over-sexed bunny.

But she didn't want him thinking she slept around. She certainly didn't. She was practically a nun since she'd opened the shop—having little time for a social life.

Someone was walking up the street. A tall dark-haired guy in a Superman T-shirt and jeans. God, he was nice-looking. As he got nearer he came into focus.

"Gavin," she breathed. Fuck, he was coming right towards the shop. She had hoped to tell him what kind of shop she had and gauge his reaction. She'd had very mixed opinions from her friends and she was still unsure which way he would tip. If the guy quoted ancient Persian kings to her, the chances were he was going to turn up his nose at knickers and sex toys. But it was too late to dash into the back and pretend this wasn't her shop. He had seen her and lifted his hand in greeting—a broad grin gracing his handsome features.

Cassidy waved back and heaved a quick sigh. It was make or break time. When he walked in the door of the shop and glanced around, her forced smiled wavered slightly. He seemed a little disconcerted—but it was a look she had seen many times on the faces of men trying to steel themselves to come into a lingerie boutique and buy their girlfriend some sexy underwear. It was a look that said *I'm out of my comfort zone.*

"Hi, Cassidy, how are you?"

"I'm fine, thanks. How are you?" *Please don't look at the back of the shop.*

"Good, ta. I wondered if you fancied coming around to the shop to help me try out our fancy new coffee machine."

"Of course she does." Danni came around to the back of the till and nudged Cassidy out of the way with her hip. They had a great working relationship and Cassidy usually didn't mind if Danni was a little familiar. "It's time for your break anyway."

"Oh but..." She really couldn't find an excuse not to go, except that Gavin was sex on legs and she doubted that would go down well with her rather too bossy employee. Occasionally Cassidy did wonder who was boss.

"Just go. And remember, you are owed lots of time. You never take long enough breaks. I can cope. And I'll be offended if you feel you have to hurry back and check on me. I have your mobile number if we suddenly run out of red PVC crotchless knickers."

She couldn't decide whether to kick Danni on the shin or to kiss her. They didn't even sell red PVC crotchless knickers, but it may be worth finding out if they were available. She shot a glance at Gavin who seemed to be gazing avidly at the cash register as if he hadn't heard. Another common occurrence among men who ventured into her shop.

"I'll just get my bag." Cassidy hurried into the back shop and checked her handbag. She quickly applied another coat of lipstick and smoothed her hair. She would have to do. Her hair was up in a functional ponytail but at least it was neat. She checked she had her phone, purse and keys before hurrying back into the main shop. Gavin was standing looking at the sex toys.

Damn!

Cassidy threw a reprimanding look at her assistant, but Danni was oblivious as she watched out the window and waved at a cute young man who was walking by.

Gavin didn't look at her but lifted an unpackaged black rabbit vibrator off the shelf and switched it on. His eyebrows rose marginally and his lips quirked so slightly she almost missed it.

"So you're the vixen who is going to unravel the moral fabric of our town with your battery-operated toys."

"They don't all require batteries." She was so fed up of defending them that she couldn't help the haughty tone that slipped into her voice. Gavin chuckled, switching the toy off replacing it and flexing his fingers. He looked at her, his eyes sparkling in merriment.

"Don't worry, Cassidy. I'm not one of your detractors. I think it's good. During a recession you have to be versatile and it shows business acumen that you've managed to tap into the market that has opened up with the upsurge in erotic romance literature."

"You seem to know a lot about it."

"I read the papers. And without knowing you, I've found myself defending your stance when people in the town discuss it."

"Oh?" That gave her a warm glow. She knew not everyone was against her. The sales figures proved that.

"We're not all small-minded individuals in Strathmorris, you know. Now come on. I have a coffee machine to impress you with. Unless you think we need one of those to froth the milk." He pointed at the large black vibrator.

"I think we'll stick to your fancy machine," she chuckled.

They hurried round to Gavin's shop. The biting North Sea wind chilled her to the core during the very short walk around the corner, but at least it cooled her down a little. There had been something more than a little erotic about seeing Gavin clutching that vibrator and Cassidy didn't want to delve into what exactly that was.

WHEN CASSIDY HAD TOLD him the previous evening that she sold lingerie, Gavin had wondered if she was the owner of the shop that sold sex toys. It had come as no surprise when his gaze had been caught by a big, bright pink vibrator.

She sat down on one of the large leather seats crossing her shapely legs and flicking back her hair. She'd applied lipstick when she'd gone into the back room to collect her bag and now she was licking her bottom lip again in that nervous gesture that gave him a boner. He thought of his old Latin master. Yep, that did the job.

Cassidy picked up the local newspaper that Gavin had left on the coffee table after reading it first thing that morning. He turned to the cappuccino machine. He had a vague idea how to work the thing and he'd set it up before going around to collect Cassidy.

"Cappuccino?" he asked.

"Yes, please."

He tried to read her tone. In the shop, she'd sounded almost breathless. Was she into kinky sex? Or at least something a bit more than vanilla. Would she indulge his fantasy? Let him try it out? Of course, he would have to get her into bed first. His cock started to harden again at the very thought. He sneaked a look at her. She was frowning over something she was reading in the paper. He took a deep breath, tugged on his t-shirt to ensure that his semi was well hidden and turned to place her cappuccino in front of her.

"Fucking old bastard!" she exclaimed, throwing the paper onto the table.

"Who?"

"John fucking Wallace MP. He's still trying to get me closed down and to bring legislation to parliament to get sex shops made illegal. I bet the hypocritical old git wrote that press release in the bed of his mistress, or just after he'd shagged some poor rent boy."

Gavin fought the urge to snort. He deserved a damned medal for not rolling his eyes.

"That's a bit unfair. You don't know him. He's got a really strong faith. That's why he's opposed to your shop selling those things."

"No, he's not. He thinks it plays well with the electorate. With all the old grannies who think that a sex shop means dirty old men and paedophiles are going to suddenly be hiding in every corner of the town waiting to pounce. People with common sense know that flashers and paedophiles are a whole different set of people to women who want a toy that vibrates once in a while because their damned husband hasn't got a scooby where to find their clit."

"Even you know that your toys sell to a wider market that that, Cassidy. Come on, let's talk about this sensibly. This MP has a strong faith and is worried about the impact. Perhaps you need to approach the problem differently and not see him as the enemy. As I said, you don't know him."

"I know he's trying to put me out of business. Besides, politicians are all the same. A bunch of self-serving hypocrites. Stop defending him. You don't know him either."

It was time for him to 'fess up. And she wasn't going to like it.

"I do know him. John fucking Wallace MP is my dad."

"Pardon?" Her adorable little nose screwed up and her eyebrows drew together as she almost fell off the couch trying to back away from him.

"You heard. He's my dad."

"Fuck. You..." She stood up and started backing towards the door. Damn, it was all going wrong and the look in her eyes told him that he had completely lost any small amount of trust she'd had in him. "So did he send you to the Small Business Association to friend me so that you could find out my weaknesses? To learn where to hit me the hardest? You're a good actor, I'll give you that."

"No. He doesn't know that I'm friends with you. Depending on if you still want to be friends with me. I argue with him whenever the topic comes up. I've tried to convince him that you're doing nothing wrong. Unfortunately, he won't listen to me."

"I don't believe you. I think you sought me out last night."

"I did. I saw a gorgeous girl who looked as bored as I was and I struck up a conversation with her. I thought she may be someone I would want to get to know."

"And you didn't know who I was? I find that hard to believe." She tugged at the low neckline of her blouse, then she crossed her hand over her breasts as if somehow covering herself stopped him seeing how attractive she was to him. He knew it was frustration. Hell, he was frustrated.

He moved to the door, essentially blocking her path and her face took on a mulish expression. But he wasn't about to let her walk out without hearing his explanation.

"No. I'd not even heard your name. I did wonder when you said you sold lingerie and that you were in the lane around the corner from my shop. I knew the rough location of the sex shop."

"It's a lingerie boutique that sells sex toys." He couldn't blame her for sounding a little prickly. He would probably be pretty defensive in her position. He began to move farther back into the shop, indicating where they had started from—the coffee area. She sighed and returned to perch on the arm of the couch, his well-crafted cappuccino forgotten.

"I know. Look, Cassidy. I'm on your side. I don't agree with what my father is doing and I've told him so. The only reason I defended him was because of the things you were saying about mistresses and rent boys."

She had the grace to blush and look down at her hands, which she started to wring. "I'm sorry about that."

He lifted her hands and waited for her to raise her green gaze to his. Eventually it happened as he knew it would

"It's OK. I would probably say the same about a politician I didn't know. I mean they don't have the best reputations, do they? If he's shagging a woman, it's his business. He's a free agent since my mum died. But the rent boy bit is mean. My Dad wouldn't hurt children, never mind pay for the privilege."

She was biting her lip. Those beautiful green eyes, with their long lashes and slightly heavy lids mesmerised him. She had no idea what that look was doing to him. He wanted to kiss her so badly but now was not the time or the place.

"I said I was sorry for that." Her voice was almost a whisper. He raised her still wringing hands to his mouth and briefly brushed them with his lips.

"Never mind. Let's forget it. We need a plan of action to convince my dad that you are not some kind of threat to the fabric of society and a plan to convince you that I'm not the enemy." He drew her up into his arms, not caring that she would be able to feel that he had a full boner now. "And then we need to find out how many dates I need to take you on before you'll sleep with me and if we can fit them all into tonight."

She wriggled against him and he groaned in sheer frustration.

Chapter 4

GAVIN HAD CHOSEN A cosy little Italian restaurant that had opened up a few months before just down the road from his shop. The tinkling jazz music, the candlelight and the delicious food all worked to help Cassidy feel as though this was a proper date. Was this a proper date? After all, this was the guy whose father was trying to put her out of business. She should feel uncomfortable. But she didn't. Plus he'd all but announced his intention to sleep with her. Which Cassidy was fully on board with, but it had kind of put the pressure on.

"I'll have the Tiramisu, please, and a mocha."

"Yes, ma'am," said the waiter in what she suspected was not an authentic Italian accent. He may have had dark colouring and the tan of an Italian, but she suspected he sounded as Scottish as she did in real life.

Gavin had already ordered coffee and a dessert.

"I can't believe you're a Trekkie too." Gavin's eyes had lit up when she had confessed to owning every Star Trek TV series on DVD plus all the movies. Not to mention her fair share of Star Trek toy figures.

"Well, I'm really mostly into Star Trek Voyager, but I have watched all the others at least once."

"Ah I see. I'm more of a TN..."

"Ma'am." Cassidy turned towards the unfamiliar voice only to be blinded by a bright light.

"What the..."

Everything happened in a blur. Cassidy still had the imprint of the flash on her retina, but Gavin was out of his seat and chasing after whoever had taken their picture. She just sat there her heart pounding as her mind tried to take in what had just happened. She felt stunned. What was it all about? Had she been mistaken for someone famous? But then, as far as she knew there were no celebrities living in Strathmorris.

Gavin returned a few minutes later.

"I'm sorry. I didn't catch him. He had a motorbike just round the corner. He was just the pillion. The other person had the bike running and ready to go."

"I don't understand. Why would someone take a photo of me?"

"He took a photo of *us*. It will embarrass my dad that his son was out with the woman whose shop he's trying to close down."

"Oh, I see."

"Yeah, he's one of the photographers for the local paper. He'll sell that to another paper and probably get a few hundred for it if they're interested. My dad will flip out and threaten to cut me off again."

"Your dad will be mad at you for having dinner with me?"

Gavin was looking around at the other diners, who, when he turned a steely glare on them, returned to their own food. It was as if this sort of thing happened all the time to him. He sounded almost bored as he spoke. "Well, yeah. It's not going to look good that his son is spending time with someone that he disapproves of. They'll want to know if he knows. If he approves of the relationship and if he does, does that make him a hypocrite? It really will be a big embarrassment for him."

Cassidy's brain was numb. It refused to take in the information that a dinner with a friend could cause such problems. Yes, she may have been thinking in terms of dates a few moments ago, but they were just having dinner. They hadn't been canoodling or having sex on the table. Mind you, the way her pussy clenched when he had absent-mindedly stroked the back of her hand with his thumb, her body was certainly not averse to that scenario.

What the hell was she thinking? She really needed to get out of this place. People were staring. And no wonder. First someone took her photo as if she was some kind of Z-list celebrity and then Gavin had run out of the restaurant after the photographer. Now she was staring at him, aghast as if he were one of the Borg from Star Trek.

"Can we just go? I've lost my appetite for pudding."

"Sure." He caught the waiter's eye and the young man came over.

"Are you okay? I saw that guy," said the waiter, all traces of his Italian accent gone. He sounded as Scottish as a plate of haggis.

"Yeah, we're fine. Can we just have the bill please? My friend is not feeling well. We'll pay for the desserts and coffees though."

"Of course, sir."

"I'll go to the loo." Cassidy really needed a minute to gather her wits. The reality of what had just happened was now sinking in. More bad press for the shop which meant another round of character assassination in the letters page of the Strathmorris Gazette. On the bright side, sales may increase but it was really tiring to be classed as the town harlot when she practically lived like a nun. Though of course, tonight may change that.

"SORRY, I LEFT YOU ALONE in there. I needed to gather myself," confessed Cassidy as she fumbled for the keys to her flat door. The door was next to the shop and the narrow stairwell separated from the boutique by an internal wall. The light was dim in the stairwell, but it was adequate for Cassidy. "Would you like to come in for coffee? I'm afraid I only have instant."

"That's good enough for me. I don't suppose you have any tiramisu?"

She grimaced. "No, sorry."

"Never mind. He didn't charge for it."

"I need to give you money since you paid the bill."

"Don't be silly. I invited you out. I'll pay the bill."

"A real gentleman. First you run out of the restaurant after that photographer in an attempt to defend my honour and then you pay the bill. What next?"

"I'll keep my hands to myself during coffee." He shut the flat door and followed her over to the open plan kitchen area. She pressed the button to switch on the kettle before taking her coat off and throwing it over a kitchen chair.

She stood for a long moment, their gazes locked, assessing one another, the evening, the day, the ridiculously short and turbulent relationship flitting through her mind. She really didn't give a crap about any of it. She wanted him.

"Really? That disappoints me."

"It does?" He walked towards her and her belly lurched. Cassidy concentrated on his soft thin lips. Almost as if he knew what she was thinking, he licked them. God, that tongue. Her mind travelled south and she wondered what it would feel like for him to use that tongue on her clit. She stifled a moan and tightened her thigh muscles. She was as horny as hell. She should have tested out one of the toys in her shop before tonight to relieve this awful tension.

He ran the back of his fingers down her cheek. "Coffee first."

Had he just rejected her? And why? He had said he'd keep his hands to himself but his body language said otherwise. She'd thought he was going to kiss her. Hurt and a little bemused, she turned to the cupboard and took out a couple of mugs. "Sugar and milk?"

"Yes. One sugar please."

"Coming right up."

"I'm not rejecting you, you know. I just think we should deal with the elephant in the room first."

"What elephant?"

"The photographer. My father. The whole mess that this is before we've even finished our first date."

"Does it count as a date if you take me out to convince me your dad's really a good guy?"

"That's not why I took you out. I took you out because I like you."

"Does it count if we don't have dessert because Strathmorris's answer to the paparazzi photographed us and you're worried about what daddy dearest is going to say?"

"We didn't have dessert because you were upset."

She sighed and rubbed her forehead. He was right and she really didn't want to deal with this now. She wanted to get naked and sweaty with him. She wanted him inside her. She wanted that hot tongue circling her nipple. She busied herself making coffee, while he stood watching, the atmosphere becoming more tense and uncomfortable.

When she opened the cupboard, withdrew a box of jaffa cakes and tossed them in his general direction. He caught them deftly and then raised an eyebrow. She picked up the mugs and stalked towards the living area ahead of him.

"Look, please don't be pissed off at me. There's nothing I want more right now that to take you into your bedroom and rip your clothes off, but I really do think we should talk."

"I'm not pissed off. I'm..." She didn't know how to explain it. She really liked him but they hadn't even kissed properly and already this was the most complicated relationship she had ever been in. "We're too different. Look at you. You're as rich as what's-his-name, your dad's a successful politician. You went to Eton. Eton for God's sake. Did you know Prince William and Prince Harry? Did you?"

"I knew Harry a little bit. Not much. He's a couple of years older than me. "

"Jesus, you know the third in line to the throne."

"Fifth."

"What?"

"He's fifth in line now. Charles, William, George, Charlotte then Harry."

She threw her hands up

"The fact you even know that is fucking disturbing."

"It's general knowledge. You'd find it on the BBC website. I bet any American could probably tell you that."

She waved her hands. "Besides the point. We're so different. I went to Strathmorris Primary, Strathmorris Secondary and the University of Life."

"I don't care where you were educated and how many qualifications you have. I like you and I don't see how your maths score in high school has anything to do with that. You're great at retail. You really helped me get the shop sorted out and I appreciated it. You made a big difference to the look of the place. I like you just as you are."

"Really, Gavin. Now is not the time to pull out the Mark Darcy lines. How will your dad react when he sees that picture and the caption that goes with it?"

"He'll be annoyed. Of course he will and I'll have to put up with a rant from him about how I'm destroying his career and any hope I have of going into politics. Little does he know that I vote Liberal Democrat. It was he who paid my subscription to the Young Conservatives, but that's not who I am. And who's Mark Darcy?"

"Do you really think we can deal with such a huge difference between us? Especially if you don't know who Mark Darcy is?"

"This is not an episode of Star Trek. We're not alien and human. Believe me, honey, my bits will still fit inside your bits."

"I know but it does sometimes seems like we're from different planets. I've read about Eton and what kind of place it is."

"Yes, it's a strange place with odd customs, but at the same point, we were still just teenagers going through surges in hormones and wanting to play lots of sport and look at naked girls."

He was staring at her so intently willing her to see his point of view. She cocked her head to the side and considered him for a moment as the tension in the room rose.

"Naked girls? Do you still like naked girls?" She leaned into him and he grinned.

"Very much so. I'd particularly like to see one particular girl naked. You still haven't told me who Mark Darcy is. Should I be jealous?"

"Do you know who Colin Firth is?"

"An actor. He was in the Kingsman."

"He played a character called Mark Darcy. I'll explain later."

Cassidy lifted her backside and pulled her dress over her head, throwing it over the arm of the couch onto the floor.

Gavin groaned and closed the distance between them, capturing her lips in an urgent kiss. There was no preamble and no more mention of Colin Firth. The need was pulsing from him as he pushed his tongue into her mouth and began to explore. Lips and teeth clashed. Cassidy wrapped her arm around his neck and surrendered to the invasion, exploring his mouth with as much desire. Need pulsed through her. She pressed her body nearer to him, until he lifted her under the thighs and moved her onto his lap.

CASSIDY WAS SLIGHTLY higher than him now and he allowed his head to fall onto the back of the couch as she became the dominant one in the kiss. She curled her fingers into his short dark hair and angled his head for the perfect position to plunge her tongue inside his warm, wet mouth again.

He ran his fingers down her back, forcing himself to stay away from the clasps of her bra. Enjoy the kiss first, his higher brain functions were telling him. Savouring her, he explored her mouth with his tongue, chasing her tongue—licking and teasing, tasting and tempting. Kissing was only ever something he'd done as a stepping stone to get a woman into bed but kissing Cassidy was erotic. He ran his fingers down her cheeks, cupped her jaw and angled her head to draw her deeper. He showed her with his tongue the prelude to the main event as he claimed her mouth, thrusting, plunging, fucking.

He was definitely going to return to this activity but for now, other parts of his anatomy were forcing their attentions on him.

His hard cock pressed against her thigh. He wanted her pussy against it. Breaking their kiss, he scooped her into his arms. She squealed.

"What the fuck...?"

"Bedroom?" he growled.

"That door." She pointed and she guided him through a doorway into a small hall then manoeuvred her through another door which she indicated and he kicked it shut. Then he sat down on the bed with her still on his lap. "Straddle me."

"I see you like to be dominant," Cassidy purred as she obeyed.

"Not in the BDSM sense. If you want another position, I really don't care. But..." He indicated for her to lift her ass. She did and he pulled his jeans and boxer briefs over his hips and down to his knees, "I'm sure we'll both enjoy feeling your wet little pussy glide along my cock."

Cassidy didn't bother to respond, at least not verbally. Instead, she wrapped her arms around his neck and recaptured his lips with hers. Gavin placed his hands under her satin-clad backside and pulled her wet pussy against his aching cock. There may have still been material between them but there was no doubting just how turned on Cassidy was. Her juices had soaked her very fancy lingerie. As the wet material gilded up and down his hard shaft, Gavin had to tamp down the urge just to flip her over and spear her. It was that image that had him ripping his mouth away from hers and cursing.

"What now?" Cassidy moaned, barely put off as she just moved her lips to his neck and started to unbutton his shirt.

"I left the condoms in my wallet, which is in my coat in the other room."

"There are some in the bedside cabinet drawer. Just check the date on them. They've been there a while."

"Thank fuck." He tweaked her bra open and let the warm heavy orbs fall into his hands. Cassidy sighed, then moaned as he circled her nipples with his thumbs. She leaned back and removed the bra. He held her firm as he dropped his head and used the tip of his tongue to flick the hardening bud of one nipple. She grabbed at his hair and rocked harder against his cock. He repeated the motion on her other nipple.

"Oh Gavin!" He sucked the nipple into his mouth, swirling his tongue around the peak, loving the way she bucked frantically against him. He suspected Cassidy wasn't all that experienced, though she definitely wasn't a virgin. She seemed to be quite shocked by her own body's reactions to him. That said, she was having quite an effect on him. He needed to be inside her.

He tugged open the drawer. It was full of detritus. A rabbit vibrator, a bullet vibrator, a bottle of lube, tampons, a book, breath mints, batteries, a sleeping mask, nipple clamps—interesting—and eventually an old bashed box of condoms at the back. He'd have been quicker nipping into the living room for his own condoms. He checked the date. They still had eight months to go. But if he had his way, they'd be gone in a couple of hours. He shut the drawer, removed one from the box and its own packet. Cassidy had climbed off his lap and was standing biting her lip as if waiting for some kind of judgement on the state of the drawer. He lay back against the pillow, whipped off his socks and grinned.

"Get those off and get on top of me now." He pointed to the wet red knickers she was still wearing. She coloured and slipped them off before climbing onto the bed and gingerly straddling him.

"Sorry, I don't normally do this on a first date. I'm sure you're used to girls who are much more sophisticated than me."

"This is pretty normal for a first time, honey. It's always a wee bit awkward. This isn't a movie." He pushed his fingers between them, finding her clit and rubbing. She closed her eyes on a half moan, half sigh of pleasure. "Are you not enjoying it?"

"Oh, I wouldn't say that. Oh, right there. Oh, that's... ah... that's exquisite."

He moved and captured her nipple again in his mouth and she moaned as she pressed herself into his touch. Gavin could take it no more. He wanted her. He broke away from her and took her by the hips lifting her slightly.

Cassidy realised what he wanted and before he had to ask or take hold of himself, she had taken his cock in hand and had positioned it at her opening. Then she was sliding onto him, her warm wetness surrounding him. As she reached the base of his cock, her hands settled over his and she flexed her internal muscles. They groaned in unison.

"God, you're so big." He raised a sceptical eyebrow at her. She chuckled. "No, I'm not flattering you. Honestly. I thought for a moment you weren't going to fit."

She looked slightly guileless as she placed her hands on his chest and started to raise herself up on his shaft. She breathed in then swallowed hard. She wasn't flattering him. He helped her, guided her in her first few unsure movements until she got her bearings. Whatever arseholes had slept with Cassidy in the past had not let her take the lead and it had been to their detriment. They'd missed out. He moved his hands up her sides, allowed her to set her own rhythm. She gazed through hooded eyelids at him as she licked her top lip. He ran his thumb over her nipple, and she arched into his touch.

"Gavin!" He thrust up into her as she slid down his shaft.

She gasped. He still allowed her to choose the tempo but he was joining in now. He needed to. His balls were full to bursting. The tension in him was like a coiled spring. He'd been a gentleman for as long as it was humanly possible. He just needed to move inside her. He needed a little relief.

He moved his hands along her smooth, silky thighs and up her sides. He wanted to play with her tits or her clit but he couldn't risk it. If he made her orgasm and she started pulsing around him, he'd come before he'd even started.

Suddenly Cassidy dropped onto him, leaning on her forearms on either side of him.

"I... can't believe it. I'm going to come... so quickly," she whispered, working her clit hard against him. He dug his heels into the mattress, nudged her thighs apart with his knees and found enough purchase to start thrusting into her hard and fast. "Oh, that's so good. Keep doing that," she begged. He couldn't have stopped if he'd wanted to. He knew his own orgasm was only moments away but didn't know her body well enough to judge hers. His cock hardened fractionally and his balls drew up. He was insane with the need to release. "Fuck!" Cassidy squealed the word against his chest, and the nails of her right hand dug into his back. He didn't care his rhythm had faltered. Nothing was stopping him now, not even the sweet pulsing of her pussy around his cock.

Gavin just made a loud shouting noise as he rammed his cock hard into Cassidy and came. Immediately his hand moved to the base of his shaft and he held tight to the condom. That had been intense and he had no fucking idea how good those things were. He'd lost his mind at the end. Cassidy was moaning and gasping for breath and he felt as though he'd been battered over the head with a blunt object.

And he was completely embedded in Cassidy.

He gently rolled them both over, depositing her on the mattress, and withdrew from her. Immediately he saw the hurt in her gaze. She thought he was leaving.

"I'm just getting rid of the condom and checking it didn't get damaged." Her eyes grew large.

"Did it?"

He tied a knot in it and glanced at it. It seemed to be fine. "No. It's OK. Where's your bin?"

She pointed to it and he grabbed a tissue from the box beside the bed and deposited it. Then he slipped under the cover and invited her to join him, chucking the pair of flannel pyjamas he found under the pillow onto the floor for the time being. He pulled her into his arms and nuzzled her hair. He felt her relax.

"I'm sorry. Did I hurt you? I got carried away," he asked.

"No. I enjoyed it once we got all our clothes off and all the awkwardness out of the way."

"It won't always be like that. We can take our time next time. Assuming you want to see me again, of course."

She placed her head on his chest and ran the tips of her fingers through the hair there. She sighed heavily. "God, I can't believe that photographer. I'd really like to see you again but your dad's going to have a fit and the press will have a field day."

"I really like you, Cassidy. I'd hate for what my dad's doing to spoil things."

"Yeah, but we have to be sensible, Gavin. There's a good chance it will anyway."

"Let's not think about it. We'll just cross that bridge when we come to it."

He flipped her over then and started kissing her. Soon he'd be ready to start all over again. But until then, he could give her some pleasure.

Chapter 5

CASSIDY ANSWERED THE buzzer and pressed to allow Gavin up. It was the night before his shop was opening. They had said they were both going to have a quiet night in alone but she'd half-expected him. He'd been like a cat on a hot tin roof. And now he stood there, on her threshold at two in the morning. His hair dishevelled, his coat open and the front of his jeans bulging.

Cassidy raised an eyebrow at him.

"Please don't send me away. I can't sleep. All I can think about is you and the opening and..."

"Did you try to sleep?"

"Yes."

"How much of this sleeping involved lying in your bed wanking?"

He frowned and looked sheepish. "If I say I thought of only you while I was wanking does that make it better?"

"Slightly. But maybe if you'd left little Gavin alone, you'd have got to sleep."

"You said he wasn't so little."

"He is compared to you."

"Why are you awake at this time?"

"Because some Tory geek boy is standing at my door ringing my bell because he can't orgasm."

"Ah!"

"Indeed." She picked up his hand and smiling to herself she led him into the bedroom. The alarm was already set. She just needed out of these pyjamas and to get him out of those clothes. Her pyjamas were off in seconds. She turned to him and noted the coat and shoes were gone. He had on no underwear, she noted as he stripped off his jeans and t-shirt.

He was already ripping the packet of the condom he had taken out of his pocket. She waited for him to put the thing on and then she approached, backing him up against the mirrored front of her wardrobe. He turned her as he captured her lips and lifted her, using the wardrobe to hold her.

She felt around for something to hold onto but there was nothing. So she moved her hands back to his shoulders. His tongue lashed hers, showing her exactly what his cock was going to do very soon. She sucked on it, clung to him and rocked against him, His cock was nudging at her—a promise of what was to come. She ripped her mouth away.

"Gavin, just fuck me now. Hard and fast against this wardrobe."

"What but we haven't... You're not wet..."

"I am. Just do it. Please."

He frowned but felt for his cock and angled it, pushing himself up and into her. When he was buried to the hilt, the look of surprise on his face was almost comical but Cassidy was desperate. She wriggled and rocked and it brought him to his senses. He pumped into her hard and fast, gritting his teeth. Yes, he needed this. It would make him sleep. She held on for dear life, aware of her own climax beginning to build but also knowing that he'd come before she'd get there. Although if she hadn't pushed him, he'd probably have taken enough time for her to come first. But it was better this way. Damn, he was good. Her breasts were aching and her nipples were so sensitive from rubbing against the hairs on his chest. She watched the veins in his neck pulse in time to his heart.

"I'm so sorry," he ground out. She rocked hard against him. She was horny but not quite ready to come. A few minutes with that bullet in her drawer she'd be fine but that would be poor form. Perhaps once he was asleep she could use her fingers but she was never much good at that. "Cass!" He thrust up into her and she could feel the warmth of his cum as it bathed the inside of the latex sheath. He continued thrusting as he muttered his apologies.

She shushed him and told him it was fine. She thought about lying and saying she'd come but relationships shouldn't be built on lies and besides, he was shrewd. He'd know. He'd felt her come already—a few times.

"Hold on," he muttered, as he wrapped his arms tight around her and turned, carrying her to the bed, placing her half on it so her butt was right at the edge. He circled his still hard cock with his fingers and withdrew from her carefully, then without pulling it off, he sank to his knees between her legs and pressed his tongue to the folds of her aching pussy.

She groaned and writhed. He opened her up to his attentions with the fingers of one hand, then pushed the index and middle fingers of his other into her entrance. She was past being polite. She started to fuck his fingers immediately as he flicked his tongue over her clit. Damn, he was good at that.

She ran her fingers through his hair but there was no purchase. It was too short. She was going out of her mind as his tongue and fingers thrummed every string of sensuality she possessed. Every part of her screamed out for release. She wrapped her fingers into the duvet cover as he sucked at her clit.

Something snapped inside her. A wave of euphoria washed through her as the walls of her pussy pounded around his fingers. She drove herself onto him as he sucked and laved at her folds and her clit.

"Oh God, Oh God, I can't breathe. You're going to kill me if you keep doing that."

The chuckle against her clit sent an aftershock through her, and she tried to roll away from him laving at her over-sensitised flesh but he held her still.

"Oh, no. You taste lovely when you've just come."

She wanted to argue. How could a pussy taste lovely? But she felt boneless. He'd destroyed her brain and her muscles and her ability to reason with his sexy ass and cute smile and six-pack and geeky ways. Oh no, talking of geeky ways, he needed sleep.

"Gavin, you need to get into bed."

"So you can ravish me again? I'm up for that but I need a little while to recover, you know."

"No. So you can sleep. You need to be well-rested for tomorrow."

He kissed his way slowly up her body and hovered above her. He cocked an eyebrow. "Was that why you rushed me to fuck you so hard and fast? Why I never got the chance to make you come first?"

"You need sleep. I wouldn't have died without an orgasm."

He smiled and pressed a kiss to her lips.

"That's very sweet but I won't die without ten minute's sleep either."

"I just want you to be at your best for the opening in just over six hours," she said, glancing at the clock.

"Licking your sexy little pussy until you scream will give me a smile on my face tomorrow that no amount of sleep could produce. The memory will keep me going. No fear on that score."

She sighed. Clearly she was talking to a brick wall.

"Well, let's get into bed and try and get some sleep. The alarm is set for seven-thirty. Unless you want to go back home?"

"No, I'm fine here. Maybe we can have sex when we wake up."

"We won't have time."

"Maybe we should set the alarm earlier."

"Gavin! No. You have a shop opening."

"Hmm! You're not as much fun as I thought state educated girls were supposed to be," he teased.

"Should you not be snorting coke through fifty pound notes and having your rich father bailing you out of jail and bribing the police not to take it any further?"

"Perhaps, but fucking working class sex shop owners is much more fun."

"And did they teach you at Eton that charm like this was the way to get girls?"

"Nah, I worked that out for myself."

He was leaning over her, palming her breast. It would be so easy to give in and start another round of love making. Soon his cock would harden and they'd still be awake at four am and five. Then it wouldn't be worth going to sleep.

"Seriously Gavin..." She removed his hand from her breast and kissed it. "You need sleep."

"I'm a young, healthy guy who can occasionally go a night without sleep. I used to pull all-nighters at university."

"I'm sure you did. But you'll be grouchy in the morning and you need to be chipper."

"And you need my cock inside you... again."

"Cuddle into me and I'll think about it, but no promises."

He sighed as though he'd been asked the impossible and laid his head on her breast. She ran her hand though his hair.

"You do have the nicest tits I've ever seen on a woman," he remarked a few minutes later, his voice slow with sleepiness.

"Is that a line they taught you at Eton?"

"No, that came out of my head. It's the truth."

"Well, not a line you learned from your father if it was truthful. We all know that Tories and the truth are strangers."

He tapped her playfully on the thigh. "Oi, that was uncalled for."

"If you say so. Now go to sleep."

"Mmm, I still want to fuck you," he murmured.

"Tomorrow."

"Mmm!" Then he snuggled closer to her, placing his hand over her breast.

Chapter 6

CASSIDY WALKED INTO *Comic Genius* just after ten the next morning and smiled. The place was buzzing with excitement and there were lots of customers. A young guy, probably in his late teens was standing behind the counter explaining something about a comic to a lady in her forties, and then he pointed to one of the areas of shelving. The customer smiled, took the comic and wandered off.

She eventually found her quarry over by the coffee machine. All the seats were taken and Gavin was turning with two steaming cups of cappuccino. He managed a tight smile as he moved slowly and carefully with the drinks over to a table at the edge of the seating area. Relief covered his features and he smiled at the cute redhead and her male companion when he placed the drinks down without incident.

Gavin straightened and looked right at her. A frisson of desire shot through her as memories of him naked and fucking her hard against the wardrobe sprung to her mind. Memories of him waking her as the alarm went off, his cock between her legs, teasing her, tempting her and finally convincing her that ten minutes wouldn't make them late made her clench her thighs together. He hurried over to her.

"What do you think?"

She had already told him the shop looked perfect. Clean, bright and inviting, with a good array of point-of-sale material. He'd struck a good balance. The front shop was a good size too.

"It looks great. I think you'll do really well here, Gavin."

"I take it you haven't seen the paper yet."

"The paper?"

"The Strathmorris Gazette."

"No. I usually don't collect it until lunchtime. Don't tell me. Evil sex fiend shop owner still selling battery-operated toys?"

He reached behind the till area and pulled it out and placed it into her hands.

"No, evil sex fiend shop owner corrupting nice Tory MPs son."

She looked at the photo of her and Gavin in the restaurant. They'd both been taken by surprise but she looked ghastly. Her mouth was open and the flash made her look washed out. She'd been frowning which made her look terribly aggressive.

At that moment the theme tune to The Big Bang Theory sounded. A couple of people reached for their phones, including Gavin. He looked at the display and groaned.

"No point in putting this off. Jamie, you're in charge. Cassidy, you're with me." He took her by the hand and answered the phone as he weaved his way towards the storeroom. "Hi, Dad, can you hang on a sec?"

They reached the storeroom and Gavin ushered her through to the office where he switched his phone to speaker. Laying it on the desk, he sat on the office chair and pulled Cassidy onto his lap. He pressed a kiss to her sweater-clad arm and inhaled deeply.

"Sorry, Dad, I was out on the shop floor. I wouldn't have heard those father-son bonding moments had I not come into the relative peace and quiet of the office. Did you phone to wish me luck on my opening day?"

"Gavin, have you seen the paper today?"

"The FT? No. Have your shares dropped again? Oh, dear."

Cassidy rolled her eyes. He shouldn't deliberately wind the man up.

"No, the local paper. The Strathmorris Gazette. You're on the front page."

"Ah, yes, I saw that. Shame. I don't think they got a good snap of Cassidy. She's much prettier in real life."

"Are you trying to drive me to the grave by gadding about town with that loose bit of strumpet?"

Cassidy gasped. "Well of all the..." But Gavin cut her off.

"Shh, now you said worse about him."

"Who's there? Who's that speaking?"

"That's the loose bit of strumpet speaking, Dad. She's in my office at the moment listening to you denigrate her for doing exactly what the Tories are always championing people for doing—being enterprising."

"It's disgraceful. Selling sex toys to decent people."

"If they're so decent and sex toys are so disgraceful, why are they buying them?"

"For goodness' sake, Mr Wallace, I'm not selling them to school children from an ice cream van," Cassidy put in. "I don't hear you complaining about the smutty magazines on the top shelf of newsagents. Nor do I remember you trying to get the video shop in the high street shut down when I was a wee girl even though we all knew they rented out porn videos. Or were you too busy renting them out yourself?"

"You watch your mouth, young lady."

"Or what? You've already tried to put me out of business. What else are you going to do to me, Mr Wallace? I don't have any nasty secrets for you wheedle out."

"Right. That's enough, the pair of you," said Gavin, gathering her against his chest as if protecting her from his father. "Dad, I'll be round on Sunday for lunch and I'll be bringing Cassidy with me. We're going to talk about this like civilised human beings. I suggest you invite Mrs Foster-Smythe. She's always been rather good at keeping you calm when you get your dander up."

"I am not having...."

"Dad, organise it, or I won't be back. Goodbye."

And with that he pressed the bit of his screen that said 'end call.'

"YOU DO HAVE A BEAUTIFUL arse," Cassidy commented as he crawled back into bed beside her. "I was just admiring it as you left to go to the bathroom."

"Should I have returned backwards so you could admire it further?" He pulled down the duvet and wriggled it. She ran her hands over it, her finger running just slightly into the crease. He nearly groaned aloud. It was now or never. "Well, what fine wares do you sell in your sex shop for my fine arse, then, my lady?"

"It depends. You may be into ladies lingerie. I suggest a larger size to fit your extra bits. Or we have thin anal dildoes, guaranteed to bring you an orgasm if used correctly. We have a number of different kinds of anal beads. On their own or used with a bullet vibrator can bring a particularly powerful orgasm."

She was still stroking his backside. He had to move onto his hip to relieve the pressure of the erection he was now sporting at the very thought.

Gavin swallowed hard, his gaze never leaving Cassidy's. Her lips tugged into a wicked smile.

"You want to try it."

He nodded.

"Is that weird?"

"No, loads of straight guys experiment. We get them in all the time. Usually looking as uncomfortable as you look now." She looked as though she was trying not to laugh at his discomfiture and somehow it made him feel better. "Anal beads or a dildo. I assume you weren't just meaning women's knickers."

"Beads."

"Do you want me to go and get them now?"

"No, it's one in the morning. I can wait."

She looked down and giggled.

"Oh baby. If you don't stop gripping your cock like that it's going to fall off. Here, let me help." She pushed his hips and he willingly moved onto his back, surrendering his cock into her hand, then groaned in relief as her warm wet mouth enveloped his erection.

He closed his eyes and gave himself up to her attentions. He had to make things right between Cassidy and his father. He needed her in his life as long as she was willing to stay.

CASSIDY SAT IN GAVIN'S Mercedes and looked up at the huge house that he'd just parked in front of. It was a veritable mansion.

"Jesus, Gavin, you could have warned me."

"Warned you about what?"

"That your house makes Buckingham Palace look like a cottage."

He barked out a laugh. "It's not that big."

"It's fucking huge."

He cocked his head and considered it. "Yeah, I guess it is kind of big. I never really thought about it before. It was just home." He turned to her and his smile faded. "Cass, I told you my dad was rich. I'm still the guy who wears Superman t-shirts and drinks cappuccinos, right?"

"Yeah, no...I'm just...I'm... Gavin, I got this skirt at the market."

"So? My dad won't be doing a label check to make sure all your clothes are from suitable retailers before he lets you in his house. It's not a designer label only sort of establishment."

She scowled at him. "Still, a little warning would have... prepared me."

"Sorry, I didn't think. If it helps, I think you look gorgeous and the skirt looks great. It looks really good quality. So, what kind of knickers are you wearing underneath?" His fingers were walking from her knee, up her skirt and towards her... She batted his hand away.

"Black lace bikinis."

"Oh, really. So maybe I could push back my seat and have you straddle me and..."

"Or maybe since your dad is standing at the front door, that's a bad idea," Cassidy interjected as Gavin leaned towards her neck, she presumed to start kissing it.

"Damn! Now I've got a semi."

"Your own fault for letting your thoughts run away with you," Cassidy said, giggling, as he opened his door.

"Wait there and let me do the gentlemanly thing of opening your door. I don't want my father thinking I've lost all my manners." Cassidy rolled her eyes but waited, taking off her seatbelt and checking she had her bag and smoothing down her market-bought skirt. When Gavin opened the door, he gave her a dazzling, reassuring smile. As he shut the door he spoke *sotto-voce* to her. "However he speaks to you, and no matter what he says, remember, you are his equal. You are not a naughty school girl here to be chastised. You are my friend and you are a guest. You are as good, if not better than any member of the House of Lords that the old blow-hard has ever had round for dinner. And you're a hundred times prettier and you are also sexy as fuck."

Cassidy gently nudged him with her elbow as she painted on her brightest and falsest smile and prepared to meet her nemesis.

"You're late," grouched Mr Wallace.

"Only by five minutes," said Gavin, pleasantly. "They were doing roadworks by the roundabout at the leisure centre and there was a big queue because they set up temporary four-way lights. Honestly we were stuck there for fifteen minutes."

"Did your sat nav not warn you?"

"I didn't put on my sat nav. Oddly enough I don't need it to find my way to the house where I grew up. I've pretty much got it sussed."

The older man harrumphed then looked at Cassidy. He was still a good-looking man in his early fifties. He obviously kept fit, his hair was dark with just a little bit of grey at the temples and his hairline was only just a little receded compared to his son's. He had quite a few lines on his brow, probably from frowning as he was now doing.

"So I take it your manners have disappeared since you're not going to introduce me."

"Oh, sorry. Miss Cassidy Moore, my umm, girlfriend..." He didn't look at her when he said this. They hadn't discussed what their relationship status was. That said, girlfriend was probably better than fuck buddies at present. "This is my dad, Mr Montague Wallace MP."

"The Right Honourable Montague Wallace MP," put in Gavin's father." Gavin gave a sigh.

"Yes, sorry. The Righ..."

"Really, Monty, there's no need to be so formal." An older woman appeared at Mr Wallace's back. The MP turned, seemed to forget himself as he smiled momentarily before frowning at the elegant woman, also in her fifties, linked her arm with his. "I'm Grace Foster-Smythe, a friend of Gavin's father. You can call me Grace, but I guess you'd better call old grumpy features here 'Mr Wallace' until he gets used to you."

"Grace," the older man growled. But Grace descended the three steps in front of the large blond sandstone house and took Cassidy's arm. She smiled warmly and gestured for them to enter the house. Mr Wallace waited, presumably being a gentleman and allowing the ladies to enter first. He couldn't be all bad. Just as they reached the door a large chocolate Labrador came bounding up and screeched to a halt.

"Oh!" Cassidy was taken aback but the dog sat down immediately and looked up pleadingly. "Is it all right to pet him?"

"Oh yes, he's a placid big lump," said Grace. Cassidy placed her hand on his silky head and stroked.

"What the hell is the hold-up?" grumbled Mr Wallace, peeking over Cassidy's shoulder. "Oh, Brutus. Damned dog. Brutus, move!" The dog turned tail and preceded them down the huge black and white tiled hallway. The oak stairway went halfway up before splitting in two. Doors came off the landing, which Cassidy suspected led to other hallways and then more stairs on each side of the giant entrance hall up to the balcony.

Light shone from the dome on the roof, and Cassidy could do nothing but stare up at it.

Gavin placed a finger under her chin and closed her mouth. "Keep walking and breathe through your nose," he said quietly, his eyes twinkling with suppressed laughter. Cassidy glowered at him.

"You have no idea how many ways I hate you at this moment."

"But you love that I'm cute and geeky and that I played along with your daft scheme to get out of the Small Business Association meeting." She looked at him and considered as he led her to a beautiful cream leather sofa in the lounge. This room had clearly been decorated by a woman. It was light and airy and was filled with feminine touches, including fluffy pink cushions. "Grace likes pink and Dad's colour blind."

"Yes, I do, so don't tell him. Gavin, I'm sure your father needs help with the coffee machine. At the very least, he needs to know what Cassidy takes in her coffee. You can go and do the honours. We'll have a girly chat."

Gavin hesitated but Cassidy gave him a reassuring smile. Grace seemed nice enough. He nodded and left the room.

"He does know what you take in your coffee, doesn't he?"

"Yes."

"Good, now tell me when do you get your new winter stock in at the shop."

"Winter stock?"

"Yes. I can't wait to see it. I really do need some new lingerie but I was going to wait."

"Well, most of it's coming in two weeks. We have the more Christmassy stuff in already but I'm waiting until after Halloween to put that out." Cassidy looked closer at Grace and just started to place her. "I know you. You come into the shop regularly."

Mr Wallace walked in at that moment carrying a tray of cups.

"You what? Grace, is this true?"

Cassidy bit her lip and her frantic gaze flew from Grace to Mr Wallace and back again. Grace, however looked completely unperturbed.

"Yes, Monty. Cassidy's shop is the only decent place in town to get lingerie. Where did you think I got them? I'm hardly ever in London and frankly, when I am, I haven't got time to be spending my time rooting around for lingerie. London is for cocktail dresses and outfits for Henley Regatta."

The men had sat. Gavin took a seat beside Cassidy and picked up his cup.

"See? Not everyone is against you, honey. Just Dad." He started to sip his cappuccino.

"Oh no, Gavin. Your father loves Cassidy's range of lingerie... at least on me."

Cassidy turned at the choking sound. Gavin had turned red as he looked from one to the other.

"You two are a couple?"

Mr Wallace and Grace looked at each other and then at Gavin and then back at each other as if the younger man was clearly deranged.

"Uh, yes, Gavin. We have been since about a year after your mum's death. We assumed you always knew." Montague Wallace ran his fingers through his hair and scowled.

"No, missed that!" he choked out.

Cassidy rubbed his back gently.

"Oh right. Didn't the fact that Grace always stays over give it away?"

"It's a huge house. There are lots of guest bedrooms."

"She lives in the next street."

Gavin blinked and then groaned, dropping his head to Cassidy's shoulder. "God, I'm so stupid. Why did I not see it?"

Cassidy turned to Gavin. "Gavin, honey, you said you'd show me that collector edition Star Trek figurine in your room. I think I'd like to see it now."

"Great idea. You like Star Trek too, Cassidy?" Cassidy nodded and Grace gave her a winning smile. "Very top of the stairs, turn right and it's the fifth door on the left. It still has a hand-made sign on it. Something to do with certain death if you enter. I think when he was a teen the smell of his socks might have killed you."

Cassidy giggled. "Seems I'm going where no woman has gone before."

"Our lips are sealed," said Grace diplomatically.

"We'll be quick," Cassidy promised.

"Don't rush on our account," trilled Grace.

They reached Gavin's room in silence and he took her inside. The curtains were half shut and the room was chilled and dusty smelling.

"You don't come home much."

"Christmas, Easter, his birthday, my birthday, Grace's birthday. Christ, she's practically been my step-mother all these years and I never noticed. Why didn't they tell me? And why hasn't he done the decent thing and married her?"

"I think you have to ask them that. But when did you become so old-fashioned. Can't they just sleep together and not marry?"

"You don't approve of marriage? Would you not marry?"

"I didn't say that. I've nothing against it and I would definitely marry if I planned to have kids but expecting others to marry to conform to some kind of societal norms is a bit old fashioned. Just as old fashioned as trying to close down a shop that sells sex toys."

"You're comparing apples and pears. In fact, you're comparing apples and cars. Not the same thing, honey."

"Whatever. I think you're more like your father than you think."

He glowered at her. "So do you want to see this figurine or not?"

"No. I was just giving you a moment."

"I see. Well, I don't think I'm ever going to feel any less foolish for not seeing it."

"Don't be too harsh on yourself. Kids see what they want to see."

"I'm not a kid, though."

"No, but the relationship started when you were a kid so you've not had reason to change it in your thinking."

He ran his fingers through his hair and looked at her for a long moment. She wished she knew what he was thinking. Then he glanced round the room before his gaze settled back on her. Then he advanced on her, backing her up against the wall.

"Did I mention how sexy you look?"

"You did actually." He started to inch up her skirt as his soft wet lips kissed her neck.

"Hmm, very sexy. You know you were right. You are the first girl I've had up in this room. This is my dream come true. I've got a boner, you're very wet. And we've already proved we can be very quick when you're wet.."

He was pushing aside the lace of her knickers and urging her thighs apart. She was torn. Her body was screaming to let him touch her but they were in his dad's house. And his dad already thought she was a slut. She let him circle her clit a few times with the pad of his finger and allowed herself a few moments of bliss then she pressed his shoulders.

"No, Gavin. Not here. Not with what you're dad thinks of me. It's not fair."

The lustful haze in his eyes began to dissipate and he withdrew his fingers. Understanding dawned.

"Jesus, Cassidy. What am I thinking? Of course. I'm being such a selfish bastard."

Cassidy leaned back against the wall heaving in deep breaths.

"This is getting too difficult, Gavin. We need to talk. When we get home. I actually thought that maybe..."

"Maybe what?"

"Maybe you were going to talk me into fucking you so that your dad would know or would even catch us."

Gavin shook his head.

"Why the hell would I do that?" Gavin asked, frowning.

"I guess deep down I still don't trust you."

"Well, that's nice."

"I can't help how I feel."

"I can't talk about this just now. Let's go down and we'll discuss it later."

"Fine, whatever." Cassidy stalked from the room with as much of a devil-may-care attitude as she could muster.

Once they arrived back in the living room, Grace pointed them to two fresh coffees.

"Dinner will be in about half an hour. Tell us about your family, Cassidy."

The discussion before dinner was about nothing substantial and during the first two courses, Grace kept them talking about uncontroversial topics. But when the salted caramel cheesecake arrived, she asked about the Cassidy's shop.

"How are the sex toys selling, Cassidy?"

Cassidy froze, her spoon halfway to her mouth, and drew in a deep breath. Then she swallowed hard and answered.

"Very well actually. A lot of people seem to appreciate having the option of buying on the high street rather than having to buy from the internet. They can look at the products, ask questions and possibly feel them if they so desire."

"And do you think it's appropriate to be selling that stuff in a shop where children are about?" asked Mr Wallace

"Children never have come into my shop, not even when I just sold lingerie. Yes, the odd toddler or babe in arms. Their parents are in charge of them and their parents know what's in the shop. Parent's know that the newsagent sells porn on the top shelf and they choose to take them in there. I don't see you causing a fuss."

"It's not the same thing," the older man grumbled.

"No, it's not. If a child looks at a boxed vibrator, they're unlikely to know what it is"

"Your toys are for perverts," the MP put in.

"Perverts? What is a pervert, Mr Wallace? Someone who does not conform to your standard of straight sex in the missionary position on a double bed? "

"That's not what I mean and you know it," growled Gavin's dad. "Don't you dare try to make out I'm homophobic. I voted for equal marriage in the House of Commons. What people do in the privacy of their own bedrooms is up to them. But selling these toys in broad daylight to the public is reprehensible."

"So if an army wife comes in to buy a vibrator so she can get a bit of sexual relief while her husband is away on a six-month tour in a war you've sent him to, she's a pervert? Or what if she's an army widow because her husband was killed in the war you sent him to? Is she still a pervert? As you said, what people do in the privacy of their own bedrooms, as long as they're over the age of consent and are both consenting, then it's no one else's business. I thought as a Tory, you'd welcome me being so enterprising."

"I just don't understand the need for these toys? Why does anyone need them?"

"Why does anyone need to wear a green tie instead of a blue tie? Why does someone need to buy an Audi instead of a BMW? Because it's different and it rings the changes."

"There are other ways to amuse oneself in the bedroom, my dear. There is no need to use these *toys*."

"Not if your fucking husband has been killed in Afghanistan. Reading Chaucer might float your boat Monty but it doesn't do it for ninety-nine point nine percent of the population. We're not all dullard Tory MPs who can't think beyond the fucking missionary position. I give up." She drew in a deep breath and turned to Grace. "Grace, I apologise. It's been a pleasure meeting you. May I suggest internet dating? You might find someone more interesting and less of a tosser. Gavin, I'll be at the car. I'd appreciate you taking me home then I'll understand if you choose to leave once you've dropped me off but I can't stay here. Mr Wallace, I'd say it's been a pleasure. But no doubt I'll be reading about your thought on me and my vile business in the paper next week. Please don't allow your hypocrisy to choke you."

And with that she gathered herself, collected her bag and jacket and left.

Chapter 7

"WHY THE FUCK HAVE YOU followed me in here?" Cassidy snarled, hauling off her coat and throwing it over the back of the couch. "I don't want to speak to you and I don't want to see you. You're a spineless daddy's boy and you can fuck right off."

Gavin stood, impassive, hands folded over his chest, his car keys in his hand. The journey home from his dad's house had been in silence, Cassidy fuming internally and Gavin driving quietly as if nothing had been amiss. His calmness had just wound Cassidy up more.

"Finished?" he asked mildly.

"No, I'm not fucking finished. Why did you not help me? You claim to be on my side."

"Oh, I thought you were doing fine by yourself. I particularly liked when you told my father he was a dullard Tory MP who couldn't think beyond the missionary position. They call that an ad hominem attack and by that I mean..."

"I know what it means. I may not have heard of your Croesus guy but I'm not an idiot. Sorry my debating standards aren't up to that on an old Etonian's but Strathmorris Finishing School for Girls just couldn't possibly have accepted someone as common as me."

"This isn't about you being common. This is about you not flying off the fucking handle and thinking before you speak." Gavin's voice had risen. "Come on, Cassidy. I want you to win this, but throwing insults and stupid comments about is not going to do it. You need to win with logic."

The anger was draining out of her. She leaned against the breakfast bar and sighed. "Logic's not working."

"Then we have to wait him out. They won't ban sex shops. He knows that. The Tories won't ban anything that makes money. They'll make enough noise about it so that the prudes will think they tried. Meanwhile you charm him as you charmed me."

She raised an eyebrow. "With a blow job?"

He chuckled as he slid his arms around her and started to nuzzle her neck. "Well OK, not quite the way you charmed me. I meant with your knowledge, wit and stunning personality."

"I see. Well I'll try. Hey, Gavin."

"Hmm?"

"I've got those anal beads in the bedroom..."

GAVIN ROARED CASSIDY'S name into the pillow as white ropes of cum streamed out the end of his cock. Cassidy eased the beads out of his body and dropped them off the side of the bed. She pressed herself against his back and hugged. He was still squeezing the last drops of his seed from his erection. He reached around himself with his spare hand and caught her arm.

"Come here, you sexy woman."

She chuckled and climbed over him.

"Are you all right? Was it okay?"

"Are you kidding? It was fucking amazing. You're fucking amazing."

She sighed and moved onto her back—away from him and looked up at the ceiling. "Good, I've never done that before. I was a wee bit nervous."

He turned and reached down the side of the bed. "I'd never have guessed. Just as well I got you a wee surprise then, isn't it? When you jumped in the shower, I nipped down to the shop. I'll pay for it tomorrow. I promise."

Cassidy shook her head and laughed. "It's fine."

"No. I won't have you out of pocket. Besides, it's absolutely going to be my pleasure." He withdrew a black sleep mask and placed it over her head. She shivered slightly in anticipation. The warmth of his breath at her lips heightened her anticipation. "You only have to say Krypton, baby, and I'll stop and release you immediately."

"Krypton," she whispered. "Okay."

"You want me to carry on?"

"Oh God, yes. But no hitting or spanking. I don't want that."

"Oh baby, I'm going to be so gentle with you, you're going to wish I was spanking you." A crackling of the bag told her he was rummaging again then a satisfied sigh. "Lie back and raise your hands above your head." She did as she was told. He lay alongside her, his hard, lean muscles stretching alongside her soft curves. He hovered over her and she was aware of his burgeoning erection against her thigh. He had recovered quickly.

He touched her wrist and then something cold snapped around it. He'd chosen the high quality handcuffs. He pushed both hands up then snapped the handcuff around her second cuff. Then he moved his weight from her. Instinctively she tested her bonds. He's attached her hands to one of the legs of the headboard that held it to the base of the bed. Gavin chuckled and caught her nipple in his mouth. She groaned and arched into his warm, wet touch. He moved to her other breast and then was gone too quickly.

"Tease," she protested.

"It was what you asked for, honey. You know your safe word. Otherwise, the torment continues." He pressed feather-like kisses down her abdomen and over her mound, granting the lightest peck on her inner labia. There was more rustling. She groaned.

Then tickling. But not the warm, wet tickle of his lips. Was that a feather he was stroking up her inner thighs toward her core?

"What...?"

His words cut her off. "There is no point in you being blindfolded if I describe to you in great detail what's going on. Relax and enjoy the sensations, my little sex goddess."

There was more than one feather or whatever it was. He'd got it out of the shop. What the hell was he using? A feather boa? As the item swept over her pussy, she knew that must be what it was but she didn't care anymore.

She moaned and bucked but the soft teasing item just moved farther away. She attempted to chase, though her bonds stopped her. Gavin moved the boa out of her way, running it over her stomach then her hips. She tried to move her pussy towards it, but Gavin put a staying hand on her and moved the boa again, this time teasing her breasts.

"You're more sensitive than I anticipated, baby. Try to relax."

"I can't. I need more."

He removed the boa and covered her, capturing her mouth with his. He plunged his tongue into her mouth, his lips rasping against hers, bruising and desperate, showing his frustration and swallowing hers. She wrapped one leg around his hip. Cassidy strained against the handcuffs as she tried to deepen the kiss. Gavin pushed her harder against the bed, lessening the strain and driving his tongue into her mouth the way she knew he wanted to drive his cock into her body.

The fantasy wasn't as much fun anymore. Not when she was out of her skin with want for him. When his mouth left hers, he moved his lips along her jaw. She had no free hands to pull him back, she could have wept in frustration.

"Gavin, please."

"Safe word or no deal."

She considered for a moment. She'd got herself into this. She was in no danger and she wasn't at all frightened. And she knew that Gavin knew it. She just wanted him to fuck her. She was merely frustrated. Her competitive nature rose to the fore and she gritted her teeth.

"You're just a little bit evil, aren't you?" she whispered.

"Only if you want me to be."

"Are you sure you're not a Tory?"

"Only the hypocritical kind that buys anal beads."

Her chuckle turned to a moan as he covered her nipple with his lips. This time he spent long minutes flicking it with his tongue, suckling on it and running his tongue around the areola. She closed her eyes and drank in the sensations. When he moved onto the other breast, he danced his fingers down her belly to her pussy. He pushed his fingers through her neat short curls and pressed her clit.

She bucked into his touch. She moved his fingers expertly, knowing exactly how to make her dance to his tune. Within a few minutes she was panting heavily and begging him. He kissed his way down her body and she held her breath in anticipation. When his lips touched her aching flesh she nearly wept with relief. He scored his tongue through her heated flesh, soothing it yet setting it afire. She tensed, digging her heels into the mattress.

"Shh! Baby. Play the long game," he whispered against her flesh. She shook her head. The friction of her hair against the pillow seemed to give her some kind of relief. She pulled at her bonds, not caring about the pain in her wrists. She wanted more of Gavin.

"Jesus, Cass, don't hurt yourself," he muttered, lifting her butt and moving it slightly up the bed before he touched the tip of his tongue to her clit and started to torment her anew. He worked his tongue and lips around her needy flesh, sucking, licking, kissing, nipping. Without the sense of sight, her sense of touch was magnified five-fold and every movement he made caused waves of need to roll through her.

She wasn't quiet. She cried out, she pleaded, she moaned and writhed under his touch. And he chuckled and groaned against her. Then he stopped and shifted his position. She thought he might be half leaning over her. A scraping noise as if he was opening the bedside cabinet drawer. Had he forgotten condoms again? Was there even any left in that drawer? She'd need to get more. Then a buzzing noise. One of her vibrators. She couldn't tell if it was her rabbit or the bullet.

When he touched the little buzzing toy to her nipple, she knew it was her rabbit. Some men were slightly worried about measuring up to bigger vibrators. Though she knew Gavin had nothing to worry him. He danced the tip over her nipple and she bit her lip. She knew where she wanted it—lower.

"Gavin!" She bounced on the bed, gritting her teeth, and his tone when he spoke was soft.

"How desperate are you, baby?"

She hesitated and considered. "Make me come and I can go on." The mattress vibrated. He must have put the vibrator down on it. He ground out a curse. Then he shifted onto his knees and chuckled. "What's going on?"

"I'm holding it between my knees. It's kind of funny but kind of... umm...."

"Yeah, I know. We can use it on your balls sometime. You'll like that."

"Mmm!" And then he touched her cleft with the cold, wet vibrator. He'd smeared it with lube and she jerked away from the freezing liquid, but he caught her hip and parted her thighs. The lube warmed immediately. It hadn't been that cold—just a shock when she'd not been expecting it. Gavin pressed the buzzing shaft against her clit. She sighed and pressed up against it.

"How's that," he asked.

"Angle it backwards. As if you were sticking your cock between my legs."

"Like this?" He moved it. God, she was so close.

"A bit harder at the front. Ah God, yes." She moved her hips, the lube making her slide easily up and down the vibrating shaft. She felt him move, but he kept his hand steady. Then again his lips were on her nipple and he was sucking. She nearly there—wanting to be free so she could hold his hand firmer against her clit.

"Harder," she ground out and Gavin reacted, moving the vibrator forward and back as he leisurely flicked the tip of her nipple with his tongue, his head resting on her chest. She could imagine him and how he would be lying with his cute half-smile tugging as his narrow tongue flicked quickly over her dark pink nub.

"Come on, Cass. You're so close, you're shaking." He sucked her nipple and pressed the vibrator hard against her. She held still and let the toy do its work. Tension filled her belly, her thighs, her pussy. She was trembling in anticipation. She moved slowly and deliberately. Gavin flicked his tongue over her nipple and sucked.

She rocked against the hard vibrating shaft, knowing she couldn't prevent herself falling over the edge. As the tension snapped she cried out, rocking hard against the vibrator, extending the waves of pleasure washing through her body, stealing her thoughts and ability to function. Pure ecstasy pounded through her veins and she crossed her legs, clinging to the vibrating toy that brought her so much pleasure, aware of Gavin holding her, kissing her neck, chest, breasts and stomach before he forced her legs apart.

She lay gasping for breath as he took the vibrator and pushed it inside her—the bunny ears tickling her clit which was over-sensitised.

"Oh, God."

He was kissing back up her stomach.

"Do you want to stop?" Gavin asked. She didn't know. Her orgasm had blown her mind, but she wanted to make love to him and she was also interested to see where this was going. Besides, the vibrator was making her want to go on.

"No. I'm fine," she said breathlessly.

"Sure, baby?" She felt the click of the handcuffs, releasing one wrist. He flipped her onto her stomach and pulled her still-handcuffed wrist behind her back. Instinctively, she grabbed for the top of the mattress with her free hand. He straddled her, sitting across her backside and reaching to uncurl her fingers. "I'm not going to hurt you. Just tie you up and tease you a different way." Soft wet lips touched the nape of her neck and he waited for her to say her safe word or to acquiesce.

She let go of the mattress and he caught her wrist, pulling it behind her back and securing it with the handcuff. "Onto your knees." She complied.

The vibrator slipped out, caught on the bedsheet as she moved. Gavin moved behind her and settled on his knees behind her, his thighs spayed either side of her—so close, her tied hands touched his rock-hard cock. She rubbed her thumb up the hard shaft already covered in a condom and he sucked in a breath, just as he pushed the vibrator back into her.

He plunged it deep then pulled it out to the very tip before plunging again—over and over again. The little bunny ears were perfectly positioned, persistently tantalising her clit and folds. She knew she was already close to the edge. Cassidy wrapped her fingers around his cock and stroked hard but due to the handcuffs she could not reach his tip.

He cursed and pulled the vibrator out. He pushed her shoulders forward so her head was on the mattress and then speared her with his cock. Gavin's groan of relief reverberated through her—much more than the vibrations of the toy still buzzing away somewhere on the mattress. Head down, hands still tied, she could do nothing but buck in counter-point to his thrusts.

"Oh fuck, Cass. You drive me to the brink." He pounded into her, his large hands gripping her hips, setting the rhythm for them, taking the lead. Then he nudged her legs slightly farther apart. His cock slid home, deeper than ever before. She'd be more likely to come that way. "Is this okay?" he asked suddenly.

She was getting close. He was hitting all the right places, his mastery of her and her body was inspiring. He had her fantasies covered but he hadn't crossed her boundaries. "It's fine," she managed.

"You don't sound fine. I can stop," he said through gritted teeth.

"Don't you fucking dare stop." Her body was tensing now. In seconds it would be over.

"Are you..."

She turned her face into the pillow and yelled his name as the flood of euphoria overtook her senses and her body. Wave after wave of pleasure washed through her and somewhere in her consciousness she was aware of him yelling her name, of being held in position and of her internal muscles clamping around his cock. Of her hands being freed and of wrapping her arm around him and kissing him greedily. And of them lying recovering in each other's arms.

"WHAT THE ... CASS, what's that?" The high-pitched squealing noise had woken Gavin and he was disorientated, trying to reach for the alarm. Despite his confusion he knew it wasn't the morning alarm. It was pitch black in the room.

"I... don't know." She sniffed. "The smoke alarm?"

That woke him up properly. He threw off the duvet and leapt from the bed, heading into the living room. Yeah, there was definitely the smell of smoke. He looked round but couldn't see any obvious fire. He headed for the front door of the flat which led down to the shop. He was about to touch the door handle but paused. It was metal. He placed his hand near it. Buck naked as he was, he had no clothing to put over his hand to protect himself. He grabbed the throw off the couch and tested the handle. It was hot. He used the cloth to flick back the little circle of metal over the peephole in the door. Yellow light was visible. Their escape was cut off.

"Shit."

"Cassidy, the shop and the stairs are on fire." He was back in the bedroom in a few strides. She was hauling on a pair of jogging bottoms and shoving her feet into trainers. He lifted his phone and dialled 999.

"Fire, please," he said as the woman asked if he wanted Police, Fire or Ambulance. He gave the details as he struggled into his jeans and trainers. As soon as he shoved his phone into his pocket, he grabbed a sweatshirt. Thank heavens he'd left some clothes here from the nights he'd stayed over.

"I'm going to get the package I keep of insurance documents and important stuff in the kitchen drawer. I'll turn on the taps in the kitchen. You turn on the taps in the bathroom. It might delay things if the fire reaches here. I saw it on a TV advert once." She was so calm. He nodded and grabbed his phone again. They could do nothing but wait for the fire service to come and rescue them. He had one more phone call to make.

Phone call made, he hurried back into the living room and kitchen area. The smoke was getting worse, which meant the fire must have climbed the stairs now. Cassidy was coughing and carrying the sopping wet throw he'd used earlier over to the door to lay it like a draught excluder. She'd opened the window and he could hear one or two voices from outside. Climbing up onto the kitchen work top which was directly in front of the window, he looked out. It was an old building with high ceilings so despite only being on the first floor, it was still quite a long drop. It was manageable, in theory. He turned and looked at Cassidy. She was calm—too calm, despite the fact she was beginning to choke. The smoke beginning to catch at the back of his own throat. Coughing to clear it he leaned out of the window.

Where was the damned fire engine? He couldn't see any blue lights. But there were some people on the street shouting up at him.

"You need to get out of there."

"Hey man, you need to jump."

"Fuck's sake, pal, it's an inferno."

Cassidy pulled herself onto the worktop, her cough turning into a spasm. He let her get fresh air. She turned a watery-eyed, terrified gaze on him. "We're going to die." More choking wracked her. He turned to look at the door. Flames were licking the frame. They needed to get out and quickly.

"Cassidy, I'm going to lower you out the window. If I drop you out at full stretch, you'll have less distance to drop. These guys will probably try and catch you. I don't know if they're sober or not but they'll probably be a relatively soft landing. I'll hang out the window like they used to show us in these old fire safety adverts. It's got to be better than choking or burning to death."

Cassidy's gaze flicked to the door, now crackling as the wood split. She succumbed to another fit of coughing. "Okay," she managed, eventually. "Do we not throw the mattress and everything out the window?"

He scowled at the small sash window. "We'd never get a double mattress through there. We'll throw out the cushions from the couch and the pillows from the bed and duvet and maybe that will break our falls a little. You get the cushions here, I'll get the stuff from the bedroom."

He moved as quickly as his feet would carry him, grabbing the duvet and pillows and even the two heart-shaped cushions she kept for decoration on the bed. They shoved them out the window and then he climbed up on the worktop and looked out. A bit of a crowd had gathered and a couple of people were sorting the pile of cushions and duvet into a suitable landing mat. He looked down. It was still a hell of a drop with not a lot of cushioning. He was torn. Where the fuck were the fire brigade? Even with him dropping her out of the window, the potential for her breaking bones was huge, even breaking her spine. It didn't bear thinking about. His blood ran cold just contemplating it. But her coughing was getting worse.

"Right. I'll hold your wrists and you need to walk down the wall with your feet. I'll hand you out the window. When you're as low as I can get you, you'll have to kick free of the wall and I'll let you go. When you land, bend your knees and we have to hope the impact's not too bad. It's your only hope."

"Can't we just wait here for the..."

The door disintegrated with a roar from the fire. Cassidy screamed and grabbed his arms, pressing her forehead against his shoulder.

"Obviously not," he yelled as he wrapped his arms around her.

AT FIRST CASSIDY HAD been numb, but now she was terrified. The door bursting into flames seemed to have broken her calmness and made her face the true horroe of the danger they were in. They could actually burn to death. She looked down at the 'helpful' revellers below and grimaced. She was likely to break a couple of bones at the least, possibly even her spine and Gavin could do likewise. The noise of the siren filtered beyond the sound of the men below yelling at her to jump. Flashes of blue caught her gaze. The fire engine was coming.

"Come on, baby. We have to go." Gavin's voice was tense but urgent. She turned and looked at the door but the fire had not come any farther. Her idea to put on the taps and soak the carpet was holding it at bay. Thank heavens for decent water pressure.

"The fire brigade are coming. The fire isn't coming any nearer." The smoke caught in her throat and she choked again. Gavin was coughing too. She hated that he would stay in the flat longer, but she knew they'd all make her leave first. Bloody chivalry and sexism. The fire engine rolled up the lane, blue lights flashing, its siren now silenced. The small gathering below shuffled out of the way as the big red truck stopped just before the shop. Firemen and women tumbled out of the big vehicle hauling on jackets, with stripes that glowed in the light of the streetlamps, the fire from the shop window and fire engine's lights. Gavin and Cassidy started to shout for help. One of the firemen looked up.

"Keep calm. Don't worry. We're coming to get you." He seemed unperturbed. As if he did this all the time... which Cassidy supposed he did.

His colleagues donned big yellow helmets. The rattling of metal shutters on the vehicle being opened, shouts from the fire officers and a hubbub of activity.

"Fuck's sake man, where have you been? Those folks are trapped," shouted one of their would-be helpers from the street below.

"Bunch of lazy cunts just turnin' up when youse like. Were youse finishin' your cuppa tea? Bastards. That wee lassie's scared out her wits. Cunts," another chimed in.

"Are there any other people in the building?" The leader of the firemen said approaching the group.

"No, just us. Just the one flat and the shop." Gavin yelled as a less potty-mouthed onlooker must have explained that they were the only people that the onlookers had seen.

Cassidy felt relief wash over her as two firemen brought a ladder over to the building and started to extend it up to the window. For all the fire wasn't getting closer, breathing was getting harder and the heat was getting worse. She noted that the firemen now had water spewing from hoses and it was aimed directly at the shop below. They were at last tackling the blaze in her shop.

A fireman was making his way up the ladder towards them. She grabbed Gavin's hand. He was coughing furiously.

"Maybe you should go first."

He shook his head furiously. He drew in a few raspy lungfuls of air, held his breath and then exhaled.

"No, you first. I'm fine." She gave him a worried look. He nodded at her and then at the window. The fireman's helmet was coming into view. His face then appeared. He was grimy, as if he'd just been at another fire. Maybe that's what had been the holdup.

"Are you both all right?" He was an older man with a cheerful-looking face, though some weary lines bracketed his eyes.

"Yes. Fine. The stairs were on fire. We were trapped."

"Anyone else in there?

"No. Just the two of us."

"Any pets."

"No."

"OK. What's your name?"

"Cassidy. This is Gavin."

"All right, Cassidy. I'm Brian. Can you climb down the ladder yourself or do you need help?"

"No, I can do it. I'm not great with heights but it's only one floor. How hard can it be?"

"Just keep your eyes on the rung at eye level and you'll be fine. I've helped people down from the eighth floor. Just turn yourself round and come out feet first. I'll be guiding you. I'm sorry I'll have to put my hand on your hips to guide you a bit, but I'm just stopping you from falling."

"Okay." She did as she was told. He had a firm grip and her foot made solid contact with the ladder rung. Then her other foot was on the rung below. She felt as safe as she could on a ladder one storey above the street next to a burning building. Gavin edged to the window and scowled at the Brian.

"Don't worry, son," Brian said to Gavin, "she's young enough to be my daughter and I treat all my charges as if they are my daughter."

And then they were descending. Slow and steady but not too slowly. She knew Brian still had to rescue Gavin and she couldn't dally. She bit her lip and concentrated.

"Don't panic, Cassidy. He's all right. Is he your husband?"

"Boyfriend."

"Well, he's not in any immediate danger. I checked when I collected you. If he had been, although it would have been more dangerous, I'd have brought you down together. So don't panic."

"Thank you."

"We're nearly there. Only a few rungs to go."

And he was right. Six more rungs and a blanket was thrown around her shoulders and a paramedic was pulling her off to the side. Of course, there was no way she was going to sit in the back of an ambulance until Gavin was rescued.

Brian had gone back up the ladder in a trice and Cassidy watched as the fireman helped her boyfriend out of the window. When she noticed the big brown envelope sticking out of Gavin's jeans, she could have kissed him. After running to fetch the insurance documents, she'd forgotten them again in her panic. He'd remembered. And now Brian's big safe hands were on Gavin's hips as her boyfriend settled his feet safely on the rungs of the ladder.

"Here, Cassidy, put this mask on. It will help your breathing." She turned to the young woman in the paramedic jumpsuit holding out an oxygen mask to her. It was only then that Cassidy realised how laboured her breathing was. "You'll have breathed in a lot of smoke."

She didn't argue but allowed the mask to be put over her nose and mouth. The oxygen did ease her breathing and she stood, allowing the paramedic to support her as her boyfriend made his way steadily down to safety. And then she was enveloped in his arms, a blanket being placed around his shoulders. Brian stood to the side, and she caught his gaze. He smiled in a father-like way.

"Thank you." He nodded.

Gavin looked up. "Yes. Thank you." He stuck a hand out from underneath his blanket and the fireman took it, shaking it warmly.

"You're welcome. All part of the job." He wiped his hand over his face and Cassidy wondered what she read in his eyes. It wasn't triumph. She wondered if he'd saved everyone tonight. She scowled and drew closer to Gavin. He had to rest his cheek on her head so his mask didn't get in the way."

A police woman approached.

"Hello, I'm PC McGuire. Are you the owners of the flat above the shop?"

"I am. I also own the shop. I'm Cassidy Moore."

"Right. And were you staying in the flat also, sir?"

"Yes. I don't live there but I was staying over. I'm Gavin Wallace. I live round the corner in the flat above the new comic book store. I just moved there from Edinburgh."

"I see. And it's only the one flat."

"Yes."

"I'll need to ask some questions for now, but I can probably ask more in the morning but we need to establish a few facts then arrange somewhere for you to stay tonight. Do you know what how the fire started?"

They looked at each other. Gavin stroked Cassidy's hair soothingly, "No. We were asleep."

"Miss Moore?"

"I was asleep too. It must have started in the shop. The flat wasn't on fire when we woke up."

"The smoke alarm woke us up and the stairs were on fire. I phoned the fire brigade."

"Do you know what could have started the fire downstairs?"

"We've no cooking facilities or fires down there so I can't think of anything. I don't use candles or matches. So no," supplied Cassidy.

"Smokers, left cigarette?"

"No, neither Danni nor I smoke."

"Anyone who holds a grudge?"

She stiffened but Gavin spoke. "No, no one." Obviously he didn't think anyone would try to kill her over a few vibrators. She couldn't even think anymore. "Can we do this later? She's shaking. She's in shock."

He'd drawn her into his side and suddenly it just all seemed too much to cope with. "I thought I was going to lose you when the door burst into flames. I thought we were going to die," she whispered.

"Shh, baby, I know." He ran his fingers up and down her spine and it felt as if he was trying to infuse the calm he didn't even feel himself. There was a tension in him that she'd never noticed before. But he was a master of hiding his emotions. He'd told her so. He'd been taught to hide them at Eton.

"I'm sorry but I still need to ask the questions." The policewoman did look like she would prefer to leave it. But she supposed she was just doing her job. "Is there a fire alarm in the shop?"

"Yes, but my risk assessment had said I only needed a very basic one. There is a smoke alarm but I don't know why it didn't go off. It's checked regularly as per the legal requirements. Maybe it did and we didn't hear it."

"So you woke to the sound of the smoke alarm from the flat. Then what happened?"

"Gavin went to check what was going on. He found the stairs on fire. I was putting clothes on and finding the insurance documents and my main certificates and stuff which are in an envelope. Someone once told me to keep them all together in case this or something like it happened."

"Then what?"

"We turned on the taps to wet the carpet. Gavin had phoned the fire brigade by then and we just waited. We were going to jump but then we heard the sirens and saw the blue lights."

"All right. I'll take some basic information about you both for now then we need to find you temporary accommodation." The policewoman smiled at them. Cassidy frowned as an elegant woman and older but handsome gentleman pushed through the crowd. She saw the man talking to the guy who seemed to be in charge of the fire brigade. Gavin's dad.

She yanked off her mask and pushed Gavin aside. "What the fuck is he doing here?" she snarled. Gavin was a few steps behind her but caught her up easily catching her by the elbow.

"Cass, it's fine."

"It's not fucking fine. Come here to gloat, your lordship!" she yelled at him.

"Cassidy, you're making an arse of yourself," Gavin hissed.

"Why? He wanted rid of my shop. This is the perfect fucking way. And now he's here. Why the fuck do you even know in the middle of the god damned night, you old bastard?" She had reached him and she was face to face with him. "Did you burn down my shop?" she yelled, her fists pounding on his shoulders.

Mr Wallace's strong fingers wrapped around her wrists and removed her from him, but he did not hurt her.

"Get a grip of yourself, Cassidy." His voice was low and menacing. "Gavin phoned me. That's why I'm here. I can help. I want to help. For some god-forsaken reason, both he and Grace like you and I'm just going to have to tolerate you and vice versa. So, before we make any more of a scene that makes it into tomorrow evening's paper, you need to calm down." He stayed her with a glare, his eyes so like Gavin's. She swallowed hard. Gavin's arms were around her and he was lifting her away from his father.

"It's all right, Dad." Cassidy swallowed again then stole a glance at Grace who was leaving Mr Wallace's side and coming towards her.

"Are you both okay?"

"We're fine. Just... shaken... you know?" said Gavin, quietly.

Grace grabbed them both in a hug. "Thank god. When you phoned, your father was out of his mind with worry."

"Now Grace, don't over-egg the pudding. I was fine. I was just... well... concerned."

Cassidy glanced at the gruff man and saw his eyes shining.

"Excuse, me Miss Moore, can I have a word?" She looked up at PC McGuire. Cassidy nodded.

"Ah constable, do you mind if I have a word with you? The Right Honourable Montgomery Wallace MP." Slightly flustered, the policewoman allowed herself to be drawn aside.

GAVIN ROUNDED ON CASSIDY. He was really at the end of his rope with her.

"You don't honestly believe my dad set your shop on fire do you?"

Cassidy stared at him, her gaze mutinous and when she shrugged her shoulders the gesture was belligerent. He wanted to shake her.

"He hates what I sell."

"He has other ways of stopping you. Ways that don't include killing his only son."

"When we left his house I was mad at you. He didn't know we'd make up."

"He didn't know we wouldn't. He's not an arsonist and he's not a murderer. My mum's car went up in flames when she crashed, you know. They identified her with dental records. But he saw photos of the crash site in the papers—the burnt out shell of her car. I think he still has nightmares twenty some years later. Our family don't play fast and loose with fire, Cassidy."

"Oh!" Her face fell. Her set jaw dropped and she raised a hand to his arm. He shrugged it off. "Gavin, I'm... sorry."

But he had turned away. The emotions of the whole night far too raw. She didn't know that all of that was a hazy memory to him.

She slid a hand slid into his. "You're right. I'm an arsehole. I'll apologise to your dad. I see all my hard work going up in flames and I can't believe it but that's nothing compared to what your family has gone through. I'm so sorry, Gavin."

He wasn't yet ready to answer. He needed a moment or two to gather himself and be ready to accept her apology. She tried to tug her hand out of her grip, assuming his silence meant he was not willing to forgive but he held it fast. Out of the corner of his eye, he saw her look up, tears shining in her big green eyes.

PC McGuire approached and addressed Gavin. "Mr Wallace has said you can stay at his house tonight. He's explained everything."

"You can organise something for me. Can't you? Temporary accommodation of some kind."

The policewoman looked confused. "I believe the invitation to stay with Mr Wallace extended to you both."

Cassidy looked up at Gavin. "Ah! I don't know." She turned back to the constable. "What's the alternative?"

The policewoman grimaced. "At this time, probably nothing particularly pleasant until we can get social workers in the morning."

"Come on, stay with my dad. He's not an ogre, Cass."

It seemed as if the fight left her at that moment as with a resigned sigh she agreed.

"All right."

"You need to go to the hospital first to be checked over."

"We'll drive you." It was his dad. "Come on."

"What happens about the shop?" Cassidy asked.

"Give me the address you'll be staying at. The fire service will secure it and they'll need to interview you too. It won't be until morning now. They'll do an investigation into the cause. They also need to make sure the building is safe before you can get in to get out any personal belongings that can be retrieved. Leave phone calls to insurance companies until after you've spoken to the fire service."

Cassidy nodded. "Thank you." His father gave PC McGuire his address and led them to the car.

"Cassidy, I think given the circumstances, you should call me Monty. All my friends do." She nodded and climbed into the back seat of the Jaguar, as the old devil smiled as if knowing that had probably been the thing that shocked her most that evening.

Epilogue

"OH CASSIDY, THIS IS it." Grace held up the ivory bustier with the suspenders attached and little rosebuds all along the heart-shaped neckline. "It's gorgeous." Cassidy grinned at the woman who would soon be Gavin's stepmother. The woman was helping her unpack her new line in wedding lingerie, ready for the opening of the shop the next day. Everyone was pitching in, even Monty, though he'd been sent round to the comic book store for coffee.

With her insurance money and a generous donation from the local community—Cassidy suspected the local community of one—Mr Montague Wallace, she'd been able to afford the lease on the shop next door and extend her stock. Much to Monty's disgust, she was still selling sex toys. But he had agreed to stop his vendetta to close her down.

There had been a spate of fires in the community. Cassidy's shop and the fire earlier that night had been the first two. Five other shops had been set alight before the vandals had been caught and the perpetrators were still awaiting trial. Cassidy and Gavin had been lucky. The elderly mother of the owner of the card shop that had caught fire the night of the boutique fire had not been so lucky.

"Take it home and try it out with your dress. If it's not right, just bring it back. We can always check the catalogues and find something similar. Just make sure it doesn't spoil the line."

"Yes, ma'am," said Grace, grinning. Cassidy placed it into a box and then a large bag just as Monty returned, balancing paper cups. Danni ran to open the door for him. He frowned at her.

"Nice dress. When will Cassidy pay you enough to buy the bottom half?" Danni looked down at her mini skirt and laughed.

"You're a right old fuddy duddy, Monty." It occurred to Cassidy that Monty had never told Danni she could call him by his first name. "That's something my dad would say. For someone bringing coffee for all of us preparing to open a knicker shop, that's pretty hypocritical."

"Only because I nearly have a bird's eye view of your knickers."

"It's all right. I'm a lady, don'cha know. I know how to bend so you don't see my bits."

"Thank heavens for that," he muttered. Danni grabbed a coffee and flitted into the back of the shop.

"She's a good worker and she knows her lingerie. And her sex toys," Cassidy said, coming over to Monty and taking the cup with a C on it.

"I thought you and I agreed about never mentioning the sex toys."

"Come on, Monty, after everything..."

Gavin wrapped his arms around her waist and pressed his warm, wet lips to her neck.

"What happened to the entente cordiale? You promised," he whispered.

"I know, I just..."

"Come, I have something to show you."

Gavin removed the cup from her hand and set it on the counter. With an apologetic look for his father he took her by the hand and led her upstairs. She had been banned from the flat as the renovations had gone on. He brought her into the living room and kitchen area. It was fancy and modern. She sucked in a breath. It looked like a show flat for a magazine.

"It's beautiful," she said, her voice quiet with awe.

"Come and see the bedroom."

He tugged on her arm. They moved into the small hall. A door now led off to the bathroom, whereas before the bathroom had led from the bedroom. He opened the door. Her room was much bigger. In the middle was a huge four-poster bed. She couldn't draw her gaze away from it.

On the large red satin cover lay a pair of hand cuffs, a vibrator and a blindfold. They no longer needed condoms, having both been tested and her now taking the pill. He was behind her tweaking the buttons on her jeans and moving his fingers under the elastic of her knickers. She arched to allow him access, with his other hand he nudged her bra out of the way and rubbed a thumb over her nipple.

"What about your dad and Grace?"

"I think when we don't go down for a while, they'll work out that we got distracted."

"Hmm." He was kissing her neck, running his tongue up to just behind her ear. "I know it's a bit vanilla, but can we leave the toys till tonight. For our first time back in my flat, I just want it to be us. No embellishments."

"Oh baby. Absolutely. I'm just a simple boy from a small town in Scotland. Vanilla's my favourite flavour. And the little sex shop around the corner is my favourite location."

The End

Don't miss out!

Visit the website below and you can sign up to receive emails whenever Em Taylor publishes a new book. There's no charge and no obligation.

https://books2read.com/r/B-A-VMXC-VINJ

BOOKS2READ

Connecting independent readers to independent writers.

About the Author

Em hails from the city of Glasgow in bonny Scotland. She works as a home carer by day and at night she writes down the adventures of young women and their romantic conquests. She loves Modern Country music, travelling, and watching dreadful reality TV.

www.ingramcontent.com/pod-product-compliance
Lightning Source LLC
LaVergne TN
LVHW040952150826
845672LV00002B/657

* 9 7 9 8 2 3 0 2 6 6 8 5 3 *